Santa

GETS THE FLU

Merry Christmas
YMardi Sucker

Brad Werren

Dedicated to...
Our Mothers: Betty Lou Tucker and Agnes Bernice Werner
Our Daughter: Amy Brice Werner
Our Grandsons: Beau Bradley Werner, Wade James Werner,
Luc Allison Werner

"Mrs. Claus, what will I do?
I think that I have the flu!
I ache all over, my head is hot.
I should have gotten my flu shot.
I can't disappoint the girls and boys.
They are counting on Santa to bring them toys.

A baby doll for little Jenny.
Shiny new bikes for Tommy and Kenny.
Building blocks and a truck for Jonny.
Teddy bears for Amy and Bonnie.
So many more, this is just a few.
But how can I do it if I have the flu?

My temperature is a hundred and three.
How could this have happened to me?
Especially at this time of year.
With Christmas Eve so very near.
I have to get better**!** It has to be quick**!**
Maybe some soup will do the trick."

Mrs. Claus put another blanket on the bed.
Then fluffed the pillow under Santa's head.
Mrs. Claus kissed Santa's cheek and quickly hurried out.
The soup had to work, but she had her doubts.
When Mrs. Claus returned, Santa was fast asleep.
She left the room without making a peep.

What were they going to do?
If Santa really had the flu.
"I'll talk to the elves, maybe they will know.
How to give Santa back his HO, HO, HO."
Mrs. Claus went down to the elves' workshop.
They were all busy working nonstop.

Mrs. Claus was spotted by Joe, the head elf.
He thought she didn't seem her happy self.
As Joe started walking her way.
He saw on Mrs. Claus' face a look of dismay.
"Mrs. Claus, why are you upset?
Is it because we aren't finished yet?

Are you worried we won't get everything done?
Because we are laughing and having fun?"
"Oh, dear Joe, that isn't it.
Is there somewhere I can sit?"
Joe brought Mrs. Claus a chair and she sat down.
As all the elves gathered around.

"I have bad news for all of you.
It seems that Santa has the flu!"
Santa sick! It was hard to believe!
There were only five days
left until Christmas Eve!
"Will he get better?" "Will he be all right?"
"Will he able to make his flight?"

Mrs. Claus could only answer, "I don't know."
"What will we do?" Mrs. Claus asked Joe.
Joe scratched his head and thought for a while.
Then gave Mrs. Claus a gentle smile.
"If it is really true.
And Santa does have the flu.
We'll find a way to deliver the toys.
We will keep Santa's promise to all the girls and boys."

As Mrs. Claus got up and started to leave.
She felt a slight tug upon her sleeve.
It was a tiny elf everyone called Nell.
"Mrs. Claus, Santa will get well."

Mrs. Claus smiled as she wiped a tear from her eye.
She didn't want the elves to see her cry.
Thanking them Mrs. Claus hurried out.
"Back to work!" Mrs. Claus heard Joe shout.
Walking home, Mrs. Claus pulled her coat tight.
Her home ahead was a welcome sight.

Opening the front door Mrs. Claus was glad to be back.
She hung her coat and scarf on the hall rack.
Putting on her old gray sweater.
Mrs. Claus hoped Santa was feeling better.
Santa was still sound asleep in his bed.
Mrs. Claus gently touched his forehead.

Sitting down in the big overstuffed chair.
Mrs. Claus wanted Santa to know she was there.
She left on a little light.
In case he awoke in the middle of the night.
The next few days passed by quick.
Santa was still very sick.

Santa wasn't happy staying in bed.
So many last minute details in his head.
Mrs. Claus and the elves were doing their best.
They knew that Santa needed his rest.
But then they ran into a little snag.
They couldn't wrap the toys without a gift tag.

Santa always signed every one.
How were they going to get this done?
Mrs. Claus thought and thought.
Then she remembered the rubber stamp Santa had bought.
Santa had gotten it on a whim.
Thinking Mrs. Claus could help him.

It was just one of Santa's silly gags.
Never intended to be used on the tags.
But now it would save the day!
The elves could start wrapping right away.
Their little hands into action flew.
They knew exactly what to do.

So many toys they had to wrap.
There would be no time for a nap.
They worked all day and through the night.
The wrapped gifts were such a pretty sight.
Mrs. Claus stamped tag after tag.
As Joe went to get Santa's big red bag.

Finally they got it all done.
With sighs of relief from everyone.
"Get some sleep," Mrs. Claus said with a smile.
"I'm going home for a little while.
I'll check on Santa and take a nap.
Then we will go over his flight map."

Little Nell whispered, "I still believe,
Santa will be better by Christmas Eve."
Mrs. Claus kissed Nell's precious little head.
And she gently tucked her into bed.
She wished she had Nell's belief.
It would certainly be a big relief.

When Mrs. Claus got home, Santa was still in bed.
Softly she put her cheek to his forehead.
Santa's fever was gone and he didn't feel hot.
Should she wake him. She thought not.
Once again Mrs. Claus slept in the overstuffed chair.
After putting a nightcap over her hair.

Finally it was Christmas Eve day.
The elves were busy polishing Santa's sleigh.
The reindeer were playing and prancing around.
The bells on their harnesses creating a welcome sound.
Santa was sitting up in bed.
Munching on some of Mrs. Claus' cinnamon bread.

Finally Santa had his appetite back.
Waiting for breakfast he was enjoying a snack.
Mrs. Claus was fixing him eggs and ham.
Fried potatoes, toast with jam.
Tucking a napkin under his chin.
Santa was all ready to dig in.

Real food again. How good it did taste.
Not a single crumb did Santa want to waste.
The twinkle was back in his eyes.
To Mrs. Claus this was a delightful surprise.
The flu was gone! Santa was well!
Mrs. Claus silently thanked little Nell.

Mrs. Claus grabbed her coat and ran outside.
"Santa's well **!**", to the elves Mrs. Claus cried.
Squeals of joy and laughter happily rang out.
As the elves began to dance about.
Such wonderful news they had been waiting to receive.
Once again Mrs. Claus felt someone touch her sleeve.

Instantly she knew it had to be little Nell.
"Mrs. Claus, I just knew Santa would get well."
Mrs. Claus knelt down and hugged Nell tight.
"Thank You, my dear. You were right.
Now go and play. You deserve some fun.
I still have things that have to be done."

Mrs. Claus watched as Nell skipped away.
This was truly a marvelous day.
Looking around Mrs. Claus asked, "Has anyone seen Joe ?"
An elf answered, "He was with the reindeer a minute ago".
As she approached Joe, he quickly wiped his eye.
"The wind sure is cold", said the tough little guy.

"I have a big favor to ask of you.
Since Santa has just gotten over the flu.
Would you mind riding with Santa tonight?
I just want to make sure he will be all right."
"It would be my honor", Joe replied.
So many times Joe had asked and been denied.

Santa always said he worked better alone.
In a gentle but firm tone.
"Are you sure Santa won't mind if I go?"
"I'll handle Santa", Mrs. Claus assured Joe.
"Now go and get ready, you'll be leaving soon."
Smiling, Joe hurried off whistling a Christmas tune.

As Mrs. Claus entered the house, Santa called out.
"What was all that commotion about?"
"It was just the elves happy to hear you are well.
Now why don't you sit down for a spell.
You have a big night ahead of you.
Remember you just got over the flu."

Santa chuckled as he did what she said.
He didn't want to end up back in bed.
Mrs. Claus brought Santa a stool for his feet.
"Would you like something warm to eat?"
"Oh, no, breakfast was enough for me.
Maybe just a cup of peppermint tea."

"That sounds good, maybe I'll have one too.
We can sit here together, just me and you.
A quiet moment for us to share."
Mrs. Claus lovingly touched Santa's silken, white hair.
Santa stretched as he muffled a little yawn.
"You know I'll miss you while I'm gone.

"But it is for a good cause.
The little children depend on Santa Claus."
"This I know very well, my dear.
But I am glad it is only once a year.
Time for us to get up out of these chairs.
And for you to quickly head upstairs.

You have to get dressed. It's almost time to go.
Oh, by the way, you are taking Joe."
"Now, Mrs. Claus, you know I travel alone."
"Not tonight," she replied in her gentle tone.
"I asked Joe to go with you.
Since you were so sick with that nasty flu."

"Okay, dear, this time you win."
As Santa kissed Mrs. Claus upon her stubborn chin.
Santa laughed as he headed upstairs to get dressed.
"Mrs. Claus is right," he silently confessed.
Santa quickly put on his fluffy red suit.
Then stuck each foot into a shiny black boot.

Next came his belt and the cap for his head.
"I guess I'm ready," Santa looked in the mirror and said.
"Oh, Santa! How handsome you look!"
Click went the camera, for the yearly picture Mrs. Claus took.
Each year the picture turned out exactly the same.
But Santa went along with Mrs. Claus' little game.

The mantle clock was striking eight.
"Better get going, Santa cannot be late."
Together, Santa and Mrs. Claus walked out to the sleigh.
The reindeer were anxious to be on their way.
"Watch over Mrs. Claus until I get back."
Santa told the elves, as Joe secured the big red sack.

Santa boarded the sleigh and Joe did too.
Both so happy that Santa no longer had the flu.
With one last jolly "Ho, Ho, Ho."
Santa picked up the reins and said, "Let's go!"

Calling out,
"I'll see you tomorrow.
Have a good night."
Santa, Joe and the reindeer
flew out of sight.
Merry Christmas!